Also by Rachael Reed

Codefendant
Codefendant
Once a Cheater
Once a Cheater
Passport Bro
What Happens in Prison
Preference
Sprinkle Sprinkle
Championship Bad
Street Exodus
Street Exodus
Street Royalty
Pawns of Power
SIS
Cartel Bloodline
Get Money Girls
Skip the Games
Til Death Do Us Part
Backpage Hustle

Til Death Do Us Part

Rachael Reed
©2024

Til Death Do Us Part

By Rachael Reed

Copyright © 2024 by Rachael Reed

Check Out More Great Products and Free Giveaways

https://tbdbpublishing.com/

Chapter 1: Crossin' Paths

Monique stepped into the pulsating energy of Club Voltage, her high heels clicking against the sticky floor. The bass thumped through her chest, the air thick with the scent of sweat and cheap perfume. She wasn't used to places like this, but her friends had insisted. She was out of her element, a diamond in the rough.

"Girl, you lookin' like a whole snack!" Shanae shouted over the music, her hips swaying to the rhythm. Monique smiled, adjusting her dress. Tonight was about breaking free from her sheltered life, even if just for a few hours.

As Monique made her way to the bar, her eyes scanned the crowded room. That's when she saw him. Rob stood in a corner, surrounded by his crew, a dark aura of power and danger around him. He was tall, with a chiseled jaw and eyes that could pierce through steel. He exuded confidence, the kind that came from living on the edge.

"Yo, who dat?" Monique whispered to Shanae, nodding towards Rob.

"That's Rob, girl. Richmond's baddest. Stay away from him. He trouble," Shanae warned, but it was too late. Monique was hooked. She was drawn to him like a moth to a flame, the allure of danger too tempting to resist.

Rob noticed her too. Her innocence stood out in the crowd, a beacon of light in the dark. He watched her, intrigued by the way she moved, so different from the women he usually dealt with. His curiosity got the best of him.

"Aye, who that fine-ass chick over there?" Rob asked, nodding towards Monique.

"That's Monique. She ain't from 'round here. Upper class, real sweet. You sure 'bout this, man?" his right-hand man, Darnell, replied.

Rob smirked. "Yeah, I'ma go see what's good."

Monique felt her heart race as Rob approached. His presence was overwhelming, intoxicating. He stopped in front of her, his eyes locking onto hers.

"What's yo' name, beautiful?" Rob asked, his voice smooth like velvet.

"Monique," she replied, her voice barely audible over the pounding music.

"I'm Rob. You new 'round here?"

Monique nodded, unable to find her voice. The air between them crackled with electricity, the world around them fading away.

"Lemme buy you a drink," Rob offered, leading her to the bar. She followed, entranced by his charm. They talked, the conversation flowing effortlessly despite their different worlds. Monique was captivated by his stories, the rawness of his life so different from her sheltered existence.

"You ain't like them other girls," Rob said, his eyes never leaving hers.

"And you ain't like the guys I'm used to," Monique replied, a shy smile tugging at her lips.

Rob leaned in closer, his breath hot against her ear. "You know, this life I live, it ain't easy. But you, you somethin' special."

Monique's heart fluttered. She knew she was playing with fire, but she couldn't help herself. She was drawn to his darkness, the thrill of the unknown.

The night wore on, the club's energy never waning. Monique and Rob danced, their bodies moving in sync, lost in the moment. The connection between them was undeniable, a magnetic pull neither could resist.

"Lemme take you somewhere quiet," Rob whispered, his lips brushing against her ear. Monique nodded, letting him lead her out of the club. They stepped into the cool night air, the city's sounds a distant hum. Rob led her to his car, a sleek black vehicle that screamed money and power.

They drove in silence, the tension between them palpable. Rob parked in a secluded spot overlooking the city, the lights twinkling like stars. He turned to Monique, his eyes filled with intensity.

"Why you here with me, Monique? You too good for this," he said, his voice low and gravelly.

Monique swallowed hard, her mind racing. "I don't know. I just... I wanted something different. Something real."

Rob reached out, his hand cupping her cheek. "You don't know what you gettin' into, girl. This life... it's dangerous."

"I don't care," Monique whispered, her eyes locked onto his. "I want you."

Rob's resolve crumbled. He leaned in, his lips crashing against hers in a fiery kiss. It was passionate, raw, filled with unspoken promises and forbidden desires. Monique melted into him, her body igniting with a need she'd never felt before.

They pulled away, breathless, their foreheads resting against each other. "This ain't gonna be easy, Monique," Rob warned, his voice tinged with worry.

"I'm not looking for easy. I'm looking for you," she replied, her voice steady despite the chaos in her heart.

Rob sighed, his thumb brushing against her lips. "A'ight then. We ride together."

As they drove back, Monique knew her life was about to change forever. She was stepping into a world of danger and uncertainty, but she didn't care. She was ready for the ride, no matter where it took her.

The night faded into dawn, the city waking up to a new day. Monique and Rob, two souls from different worlds, were now bound together by fate. And as they held each other tight, they knew that their story was just beginning, a tale of love and survival in a world that showed no mercy.

Chapter 2: Forbidden Love

Monique lay on her bed, staring at the ceiling, her phone clutched tightly in her hand. She knew her family would freak if they knew she was texting Rob. But she couldn't help herself. Every message from him made her heart race.

Rob: U up?

Monique: Yeah, can't sleep.

Rob: Wanna see u.

Monique: When?

Rob: Now. Meet me by da park.

Monique's heart pounded as she read the message. She glanced at the clock. 2 AM. She knew she was playing with fire, but she couldn't resist. She needed to see him. Quietly, she slipped out of bed, grabbed her jacket, and snuck out the back door.

The park was dark, the only light coming from the flickering streetlamps. She spotted Rob leaning against his car, his silhouette blending into the night. He looked up, his face breaking into a grin as he saw her.

"Aye, girl, you lookin' fine," Rob said, pulling her into a tight embrace.

Monique melted into his arms, feeling safe and alive all at once. "You crazy, you know that?"

"Crazy 'bout you," he whispered, kissing her softly.

They sat in his car, talking for hours about their dreams, fears, and everything in between. Monique loved these stolen moments, away from the prying eyes of her family and friends. But the danger was always lurking, a shadow over their love.

"Yo, Monique, you ever think 'bout what we doin'? I mean, this shit ain't easy," Rob said, his voice serious.

"I know, but I can't help it. I love you, Rob," Monique replied, her eyes pleading.

"I love you too, but this life... it ain't for you," Rob said, his hand brushing her cheek.

"Don't say that. We can make it work," she insisted, her voice cracking with emotion.

Rob sighed, pulling her close. "A'ight, but you gotta be careful. My world... it's dangerous."

Monique nodded, knowing he was right. But she was willing to take the risk. For him.

Their nights were filled with passion and stolen kisses, their days with secrecy and lies. Monique's friends noticed the change in her, the way she always seemed distracted, sneaking off to take calls.

"Girl, who you been messin' with?" Shanae asked one afternoon.

"N-no one. Just busy, you know," Monique stammered, avoiding eye contact.

"Busy my ass. You better not be messin' with no thug," Shanae warned, her eyes narrowing.

Monique's heart raced. She knew she was in deep, but she couldn't stop. Rob was her everything.

One night, as they lay tangled in each other's arms, Rob's phone buzzed. He glanced at it, his expression darkening.

"What's wrong?" Monique asked, sensing the tension.

"Business. Gotta handle somethin'," he replied, slipping out of bed.

Monique watched him dress, worry gnawing at her. She knew his "business" often meant trouble. "Be careful, okay?"

"Always," he said, kissing her forehead before slipping into the night.

Monique lay awake, her mind racing with fears and doubts. She loved Rob, but his world was pulling her into a darkness she wasn't sure she could handle.

The next day, Monique's mother cornered her in the kitchen. "Monique, we need to talk."

"About what?" Monique asked, her heart sinking.

"Your behavior. You've been sneaking around, lying. What is going on?" her mother demanded, her voice stern.

Monique took a deep breath, knowing the moment of truth had come. "Mom, I'm seeing someone. His name is Rob."

Her mother's face paled. "Rob? That thug from the streets? Monique, you can't be serious!"

"I love him, Mom. You don't understand," Monique pleaded, tears welling up in her eyes.

"Understand? You think I don't see what you're doing? You're throwing your life away for some criminal!" her mother shouted, her voice echoing through the house.

"I'm not throwing anything away. Rob loves me. He makes me feel alive," Monique insisted, her voice breaking.

"Alive? He's dragging you into his dangerous world. You'll end up hurt or worse!" her mother warned, her eyes filled with fear.

"I don't care! I love him, and nothing you say will change that," Monique cried, running out of the house, tears streaming down her face.

She found herself at Rob's place, his arms wrapping around her as she sobbed. "What's wrong, baby?" he asked, his voice gentle.

"My mom... she found out. She hates us, hates you," Monique said, her voice trembling.

Rob's jaw tightened. "Ain't nobody gonna tear us apart. You hear me? We in this together."

Monique nodded, her tears soaking his shirt. She knew their love was forbidden, but she couldn't walk away. She was in too deep.

As the weeks passed, Monique's world grew darker. Rob's dangerous lifestyle began to seep into her life, bringing with it threats and violence. She found herself constantly looking over her shoulder, fearing for her safety.

One night, as they lay in bed, Rob's phone rang. He answered, his face growing grim. "A'ight, I'll be there."

"What is it?" Monique asked, sensing trouble.

"Shit goin' down. Rival gang makin' moves. Gotta handle it," Rob said, grabbing his gun.

"Be careful," Monique whispered, fear gripping her heart.

Rob kissed her, his eyes filled with determination. "I will. Stay inside, lock the doors."

Monique watched him leave, her heart heavy with worry. She knew their love was a dangerous game, but she couldn't walk away. She was bound to him, for better or worse.

The night stretched on, the tension in the air palpable. Monique paced the apartment, praying for Rob's safe return. Hours passed, each one feeling like an eternity.

Finally, the door burst open, and Rob stumbled in, blood staining his shirt. Monique's heart stopped. "Rob! What happened?"

"Got into it with them fools. They ain't playin'. We gotta be careful," he said, collapsing onto the couch.

Monique rushed to his side, her hands trembling as she tried to tend to his wounds. "I can't lose you, Rob. I just can't."

"You won't, baby. I ain't goin' nowhere," he said, his voice weak but determined.

As the dawn broke, Monique realized just how deep she was in. Their love was a forbidden flame, burning bright and dangerous. She knew the road ahead would be filled with trials and pain, but she was willing to face it. For him. For their love.

And as she held Rob close, she vowed to stay by his side, no matter what. Their love was a risky gamble, but it was one she was willing to take. Because in the end, love was all they had.

Chapter 3: Family Backlash

Monique stood in the middle of her parents' living room, her heart pounding in her chest. Her mother, Denise, was pacing back and forth, her face twisted with anger and disbelief. Her father, Harold, sat in his armchair, his expression one of disappointment and confusion.

"Monique, what the hell were you thinkin'?" Denise shouted, her voice echoing through the house. "Rob? That thug from the streets? You lost yo' damn mind?"

"Mama, I love him. You don't understand," Monique pleaded, tears welling up in her eyes.

"Understand? Understand what? That you throwin' yo' life away for some criminal? You gonna end up dead or in jail, girl!" Denise's voice broke, tears of frustration streaming down her face.

"Mama, it's not like that. Rob loves me. He makes me feel alive," Monique insisted, her voice trembling.

"Alive? You think this is livin'? Sneakin' around, lyin' to us? This ain't you, Monique. This ain't how we raised you," Harold finally spoke, his voice heavy with disappointment.

Monique's heart ached at the pain in her father's eyes. "Daddy, please. Just try to see it from my side."

"No. You need to see it from ours," Denise snapped. "You got a choice to make, Monique. You leave Rob, or you leave this family. We ain't gonna watch you destroy yo'self."

Monique felt her world crumble. She loved her family, but she couldn't let go of Rob. "I can't leave him, Mama. I love him too much."

"Then you leave us no choice. You want him? Fine. But don't come back here expectin' our support. You on yo' own," Denise said, her voice cold and final.

Monique's heart shattered. She looked at her parents one last time, tears streaming down her face. "I'm sorry," she whispered before turning and walking out the door, her world crashing down around her.

She drove to Rob's place, her mind a whirlwind of emotions. When she arrived, he was waiting for her on the porch, his expression worried.

"What happened?" he asked, pulling her into his arms.

"They found out. They... they told me to choose. I chose you," Monique sobbed, burying her face in his chest.

Rob held her tight, his heart aching for her. "I'm sorry, baby. I know this ain't easy."

Monique pulled back, her eyes fierce with determination. "I'm in this, Rob. For better or worse. I ain't lookin' back."

Rob nodded, respect and love shining in his eyes. "A'ight then. We ride together."

The days that followed were a blur of adjustments and new realities. Monique moved in with Rob, leaving her old life behind. She was thrust into a world of danger and excitement, a stark contrast to her sheltered upbringing.

She quickly learned that being with Rob meant constantly looking over her shoulder. His enemies were everywhere, and the threat of violence was always present. She watched as Rob conducted his business, the ruthless efficiency with which he operated both terrifying and fascinating her.

One night, as they lay in bed, Rob's phone rang. He answered, his expression darkening.

"What is it?" Monique asked, sensing trouble.

"Got some heat comin' our way. Rival gang makin' moves. We gotta be ready," Rob said, his voice grim.

Monique's heart raced. "What can I do?"

"Stay close. Don't go nowhere without me or one of my boys," Rob instructed, his eyes filled with worry.

Monique nodded, determination steeling her nerves. "I ain't scared. I can handle it."

Rob pulled her close, kissing her forehead. "You a strong woman, Monique. But this life... it ain't for the faint of heart."

As the weeks turned into months, Monique adapted to her new reality. She learned to navigate the treacherous waters of Rob's world, her love for him driving her forward. She faced danger head-on, her resolve unwavering.

One night, as they sat on the porch, the city lights flickering in the distance, Rob took her hand. "You ever regret it? Choosin' me?"

Monique shook her head, her eyes filled with love. "Never. You my ride or die, Rob. I knew what I was gettin' into."

Rob smiled, pride and love swelling in his chest. "I don't deserve you, but I'm damn glad I got you."

Monique leaned in, kissing him softly. "We in this together. Ain't nothin' gonna tear us apart."

But the shadows of their world were always lurking, waiting to pounce. Monique knew their love would be tested, that the road ahead would be fraught with danger. But she was ready, willing to face whatever came their way.

As they held each other under the stars, the future uncertain but their love strong, Monique couldn't help but feel a sense of foreboding. She knew the stakes were high, that their love would be tested in ways she couldn't yet imagine.

And as the night stretched on, the city alive with the hum of danger and excitement, Monique vowed to stay by Rob's side, no matter what. For in this world of shadows and violence, their love was the only light she had. And she would fight to keep it burning, come what may.

Chapter 4: The Hustler's Wife

Monique sat on the edge of the bed, the early morning light filtering through the blinds. She glanced around Rob's apartment, now their apartment, feeling a mix of excitement and unease. The sleek furniture and luxurious decor were a far cry from her old life, but it was the unspoken tension in the air that made her uneasy. She had traded the safety of her parents' home for the allure of Rob's world, and now there was no turning back.

Rob stirred beside her, his arm draping over her waist. "Morning, beautiful," he murmured, his voice husky from sleep.

Monique smiled, running her fingers through his hair. "Morning."

"Wassup with you? You lookin' worried," Rob said, propping himself up on one elbow.

"Just... thinking," Monique replied, her eyes meeting his. "This life, it's a lot to take in."

Rob nodded, understanding. "I get it. But you got me, a'ight? We in this together."

Monique leaned in, kissing him softly. "I know. Just gotta get used to it, I guess."

The days passed in a blur of luxury and danger. Monique found herself caught up in the thrill of fast money, expensive clothes, and exclusive parties. Rob's world was intoxicating, a whirlwind of excitement and adrenaline. But beneath the glamour lay a dark undercurrent that she couldn't ignore.

One afternoon, Monique sat in the living room, flipping through a magazine. The door burst open, and Rob stormed in, his face a mask of anger. "Damn fools tried to hit one of my spots," he growled, pacing back and forth.

"What happened?" Monique asked, her heart pounding.

"Rival crew makin' moves. Gotta handle it," Rob replied, his eyes blazing with fury.

Monique felt a chill run down her spine. "Be careful, Rob."

He stopped, his expression softening as he looked at her. "Always am. But you gotta be ready. Things could get ugly."

Monique nodded, trying to suppress the fear gnawing at her. She had chosen this life, and now she had to live with the consequences.

The excitement of Rob's world was a double-edged sword. She loved the rush, the feeling of being alive in a way she had never experienced before. But the constant threat of violence, the knowledge that any moment could bring danger, was always lurking in the back of her mind.

One night, Monique accompanied Rob to a club downtown. The place was packed, the air thick with the scent of sweat and smoke. Rob's crew surrounded them, a wall of protection in the chaotic crowd.

Monique sipped her drink, her eyes scanning the room. She spotted a group of men in the corner, their eyes locked on Rob. "Who are they?" she asked, leaning in close to Rob.

"Trouble," Rob replied, his jaw tight. "Stay close."

The night wore on, tension simmering just below the surface. Monique tried to enjoy herself, but she couldn't shake the feeling of impending doom. She clung to Rob, his presence both a comfort and a reminder of the danger they faced.

Suddenly, a fight broke out near the bar. Glass shattered, and shouts filled the air. Rob pushed Monique behind him, his hand reaching for the gun tucked in his waistband. "Stay down!" he ordered, his voice cutting through the chaos.

Monique crouched behind a table, her heart racing. She watched as Rob and his crew moved with practiced precision, their movements fluid and deadly. The fight was over as quickly as it had started, the rival crew retreating into the night.

Rob returned to her side, his eyes scanning her for any sign of injury. "You a'ight?" he asked, his voice rough with concern.

Monique nodded, her hands trembling. "Yeah. I'm fine."

Rob pulled her into his arms, his grip tight. "I'm sorry you had to see that. This life... it's not easy."

"I know," Monique whispered, her voice shaky. "But I'm with you, Rob. No matter what."

The weeks that followed were a rollercoaster of highs and lows. Monique found herself drawn deeper into Rob's world, the lines between right and wrong blurring. She loved the thrill, the sense of being part of something bigger than herself. But the constant danger, the feeling of walking a tightrope, was wearing on her.

One evening, Monique sat on the balcony, staring out at the city skyline. Rob joined her, a bottle of champagne in hand. "Penny for your thoughts," he said, handing her a glass.

Monique took a sip, her eyes distant. "Just... wondering how long we can keep this up. Feels like we're living on borrowed time."

Rob nodded, his expression serious. "I think 'bout that too. But we gotta take it day by day. Can't let the fear control us."

Monique sighed, leaning her head on his shoulder. "I just want us to be safe. To have a future."

"We will," Rob promised, his voice filled with determination. "We'll make it through. Together."

As they sat in the fading light, Monique felt a sense of calm wash over her. She knew the road ahead would be fraught with danger and uncertainty, but she was ready to face it. For Rob, for their love, for the life they were building together.

The night deepened, the city below them a glittering sea of lights. Monique closed her eyes, taking a deep breath. She had chosen this life, with all its highs and lows. And she would stand by Rob's side, no matter what.

But in the back of her mind, the shadow of doubt lingered. The feeling of impending doom was never far away, a constant reminder of the price they might have to pay. And as the stars twinkled overhead, Monique couldn't help but wonder how long their luck would hold.

Chapter 5: Unholy Matrimony

Monique couldn't believe it. Rob was down on one knee, a diamond ring glittering in his hand, and the world around her seemed to stop. They were at their favorite spot, a rooftop overlooking the city, where they often came to escape the chaos below.

"Monique, will you marry me?" Rob's voice was soft, but there was a fierce determination in his eyes.

Tears welled up in Monique's eyes as she nodded, unable to find her voice. "Yes, Rob. Yes, I'll marry you," she finally whispered, her heart bursting with love and fear.

Rob slipped the ring onto her finger and stood, pulling her into a passionate kiss. The city lights twinkled around them, a stark contrast to the darkness they knew was lurking in their lives.

The news of their engagement spread quickly. Monique's friends were divided, some thrilled for her, others worried about the life she was committing to. Her family, however, was anything but supportive. Denise and Harold were devastated, their anger and disappointment evident every time they spoke to her.

"Monique, this is a mistake," Denise pleaded over the phone. "You don't know what you're getting into."

"I know exactly what I'm getting into, Mama. I love him, and he loves me," Monique replied, trying to keep her voice steady.

"You're throwing your life away for a thug. This isn't what we wanted for you," Harold added, his voice thick with disappointment.

"I'm not throwing anything away. I'm choosing my own path. I'm happy, and that should be enough," Monique insisted, her heart aching at their disapproval.

The day of the wedding arrived, and it was a spectacle like no other. Monique had always dreamed of a beautiful, elegant ceremony, and despite the chaos surrounding their lives, Rob was determined to give her just that. But it was a delicate balance between Monique's dreams and Rob's street connections.

The venue was a lavish mansion on the outskirts of the city, its grandeur juxtaposed against the gritty reality of their lives. Monique's dress was a vision of white lace and satin, a stark contrast to the dark world she had chosen to embrace. Rob looked sharp in his tailored suit, his presence commanding respect from everyone around.

As Monique walked down the aisle, her heart pounded in her chest. She saw the mix of faces – her family's stern expressions, her friends' hopeful smiles, and Rob's crew, ever watchful and alert. The tension was palpable, a reminder that their love existed in a world fraught with danger.

The ceremony itself was chaotic, a blend of elegance and street life. The priest, a childhood friend of Rob's who had turned his life around, spoke solemnly of love and commitment. But the guests were a mix of Monique's upper-class family and friends, and Rob's rough, street-hardened crew. The contrast was stark and unsettling.

Vows were exchanged, promises made amidst the chaos. "I, Monique, take you, Rob, to be my lawfully wedded husband. To have and to hold, in sickness and in health, for richer or poorer, till death do us part," Monique said, her voice steady despite the turmoil inside her.

"I, Rob, take you, Monique, to be my lawfully wedded wife. To protect and love, through thick and thin, till death do us part," Rob echoed, his eyes locked onto hers with an intensity that made her heart race.

As they were pronounced husband and wife, cheers erupted, but there was an underlying tension that couldn't be ignored. Monique's parents remained stoic, their disapproval a weight on her heart. But she pushed it aside, focusing on the man she loved, the man she had chosen to spend her life with.

The reception was a wild affair, a blend of high society and street life. The food was exquisite, the decorations lavish, but the atmosphere was charged with a sense of unease. Monique danced with Rob, their movements fluid and synchronized, but she couldn't shake the feeling that they were dancing on the edge of a precipice.

As the night wore on, tensions began to flare. A drunken guest from Rob's side started a fight with one of Monique's cousins, the clash of their worlds erupting in violence. Rob's crew quickly intervened, breaking up the fight and escorting the troublemakers out, but the damage was done. The rift between Monique's family and her new life widened even further.

Monique found herself in a quiet corner, trying to catch her breath. Rob joined her, concern etched on his face. "You a'ight, baby?"

Monique nodded, but her eyes betrayed her worry. "It's just... this is hard, Rob. I love you, but this life... it's a lot."

Rob pulled her close, his lips brushing against her forehead. "I know, baby. But we gonna make it. Together. You and me against the world."

Monique leaned into him, finding comfort in his strength. "I just hope it's enough."

The night ended in a blur of dancing and celebration, but the tension never fully dissipated. Monique lay in bed that night, Rob's arms wrapped around her, and stared at the ceiling. She had made her choice, and she would stand by it. But the feeling of impending doom lingered, a shadow over their newfound happiness.

As she drifted off to sleep, Monique couldn't shake the sense that their love, while strong, was built on a foundation that could crumble at any moment. The road ahead was uncertain, filled with danger and challenges. But she was ready to face it, for better or worse, till death do them part.

Chapter 6: Trouble in Paradise

Monique woke up to the sound of her phone buzzing incessantly on the nightstand. She groaned and reached for it, squinting at the screen. The texts were from Shanae.

"Girl, you seein' this? Smh. Meet me at D's Cafe."

Monique sighed, a sense of dread settling in her stomach. She kissed Rob's cheek softly and slipped out of bed, careful not to wake him. She dressed quickly and headed out, the early morning sun casting long shadows on the deserted streets.

At D's Cafe, Shanae was already waiting, her face set in a worried frown. "Monique, you gotta see this," she said, sliding her phone across the table.

Monique glanced at the screen, her heart sinking. There were photos of Rob with another woman, some scantily clad chick hanging all over him. The captions were brutal, full of gossip and sneering comments.

"Who's that?" Monique asked, her voice trembling.

"Her name's Tasha. Word is, she's been sniffin' around Rob for a minute now," Shanae explained, her eyes full of pity.

Monique's mind raced. She knew Rob had a past, but this... this felt like a slap in the face. She felt the weight of their marriage pressing down on her, the fairy tale starting to crack.

Later that night, Monique confronted Rob. "Rob, who the hell is Tasha?"

Rob looked up from his phone, his eyes narrowing. "Why you askin' 'bout her?"

"I saw the pictures, Rob. She's all over you. What the hell is goin' on?" Monique demanded, her voice rising.

Rob sighed, rubbing his temples. "She's nobody, Monique. Just some girl tryin' to start shit. You know how it is."

Monique shook her head, tears stinging her eyes. "It don't look like nothin'. It looks like you cheatin' on me."

Rob stood, crossing the room in two quick strides. He grabbed Monique's shoulders, his grip firm but not painful. "I ain't cheatin' on you. You my wife, Monique. Don't let them bitches get in your head."

Monique pulled away, her heart aching. "I want to believe you, Rob. But this life... it's too much."

Rob's face softened. He cupped her cheek, his thumb brushing away a tear. "I love you, Monique. We gonna get through this. Don't let them hoes tear us apart."

Monique nodded, but the doubt lingered in her mind. She wanted to trust him, but the dark shadows of his world were closing in on her.

The following weeks were a blur of tension and whispered conversations. Monique heard the gossip, the sneers and side-eyes from women who saw her as nothing more than a trophy. She faced threats from rival dealers who saw her as Rob's weakness.

One night, as Monique was leaving a friend's house, she felt a presence behind her. She turned, her heart racing, and saw two men approaching. They were rough, their eyes cold and predatory.

"Aye, you Rob's girl, ain't you?" one of them sneered.

Monique tried to keep her voice steady. "Yeah. What of it?"

The men laughed, a sound that sent chills down her spine. "He pissed off the wrong people. Now you gonna pay for it."

Before Monique could react, one of the men grabbed her arm, pulling her close. She struggled, fear flooding her senses. "Let me go!"

Suddenly, a car screeched to a halt nearby, and Rob's crew jumped out, guns drawn. The men released Monique and fled into the night. One of Rob's men, Darnell, rushed to her side. "You a'ight, Monique?"

Monique nodded, her body shaking. "Yeah. Thanks."

Darnell escorted her home, where Rob was waiting, his face a mask of rage and worry. "What happened?" he demanded.

Monique recounted the incident, her voice trembling. Rob's expression darkened with every word. "I'll take care of it. Nobody messes with my wife."

Monique's heart ached as she saw the anger in Rob's eyes. She knew his world was dangerous, but she hadn't fully grasped the extent of it until now. She felt like she was drowning in a sea of threats and violence, the fairy tale romance slipping further away.

The next day, Monique was at the salon, trying to distract herself with some pampering. The women around her were gossiping, their voices a constant buzz in her ears. She heard snippets of conversations about Rob, about his business, about the danger he brought into their lives.

"Ain't no way she gonna last," one woman said, her voice dripping with disdain. "Rob's girls never do."

Monique clenched her fists, trying to block out the words. She knew she was different, that her love for Rob was real. But the doubt gnawed at her, a constant reminder of the precariousness of their situation.

That night, as Monique lay in bed next to Rob, she felt a sense of foreboding. She turned to him, her voice barely a whisper. "Rob, what if this is too much? What if we can't make it?"

Rob pulled her close, his arms strong and reassuring. "We gonna make it, Monique. I promise you that. You just gotta trust me."

Monique closed her eyes, willing herself to believe him. But the shadows of doubt lingered, a dark cloud over their love.

The days turned into weeks, and the tension only grew. Monique faced more threats, more gossip, more jealousy. She felt like she was living in a nightmare, her fairy tale crumbling under the weight of Rob's business.

One evening, as they sat in their living room, the door burst open and one of Rob's men stumbled in, blood streaming down his face. "Boss, we got trouble," he gasped.

Rob sprang to his feet, grabbing his gun. "Monique, stay here," he ordered, his voice steely.

Monique watched in horror as Rob and his men rushed out, the sound of gunfire echoing in the night. She sat alone in the dark, her heart pounding, the reality of her life crashing down around her.

As the night stretched on, Monique knew that the trouble in their paradise was far from over. The shadows were closing in, and she was caught in the middle, fighting to hold on to the love that had brought her into this world.

And as she waited for Rob's return, the fear and uncertainty gnawing at her, Monique couldn't help but wonder how much longer their love could withstand the darkness that threatened to consume them both.

Chapter 7: Baby Mama Drama

Monique sat in the living room, her nerves on edge. She had heard the whispers, the gossip, but she hadn't wanted to believe it. Now, with Latoya's name on everyone's lips, she couldn't ignore it any longer. Rob's past was coming back to haunt them, and it was tearing her apart.

The front door swung open, and Rob stepped inside, his face set in a scowl. "What's goin' on, Monique?"

Monique stood, crossing her arms over her chest. "We need to talk, Rob. What's this I'm hearin' about Latoya?"

Rob's expression darkened. "Ain't nothin' to talk 'bout. She just tryin' to start some shit."

Monique's eyes blazed with anger. "Startin' shit? She sayin' you neglectin' your child, Rob! Is it true?"

Rob sighed, running a hand over his face. "Monique, it ain't like that. I take care of my kid. Latoya just want money, that's all."

"Money? This about more than money, Rob. It's about you bein' a father. You even see your kid?" Monique's voice trembled with emotion.

Rob stepped closer, his jaw tight. "I do what I can. But Latoya, she always tryna make it hard for me. You gotta believe me."

Monique shook her head, tears stinging her eyes. "I wanna believe you, Rob. But this, it's too much. I'm tired of the drama, tired of always wonderin' what's next."

Rob reached out, his hand resting on her cheek. "I love you, Monique. Don't let this come between us."

Monique closed her eyes, leaning into his touch. "I love you too, Rob. But somethin' gotta change. I can't keep livin' like this."

The days that followed were tense, filled with heated arguments and cold silences. Monique's jealousy and insecurity grew, fueled by the constant presence of Latoya in their lives. She felt like she was losing Rob, piece by piece, to the ghosts of his past.

One afternoon, as Monique was walking back from the store, she saw Latoya standing outside their building. Her heart sank. She knew this confrontation was inevitable.

"What you doin' here, Latoya?" Monique asked, her voice steady despite the anger boiling inside her.

Latoya smirked, her eyes full of disdain. "Just makin' sure Rob know he got responsibilities. You think you can just take him and forget 'bout his kid?"

Monique clenched her fists. "Rob take care of his kid. You just tryna stir shit up."

"Stir shit up? Girl, you don't know nothin'. Rob always been a deadbeat. You just blind 'cause you love him," Latoya spat, her voice dripping with venom.

Monique's vision blurred with tears. "You don't know what we got. Rob loves me, and I love him. You just bitter 'cause he moved on."

Latoya laughed, a harsh, grating sound. "Moved on? He ain't never gonna move on from me. I'm the mother of his child. You just a side piece."

Monique snapped, her emotions boiling over. She lunged at Latoya, pushing her back against the wall. "Don't you ever talk 'bout me like that! You don't know nothin' 'bout what we got!"

Before things could escalate further, Rob appeared, his face a mask of fury. "What the hell is goin' on here?"

Monique stepped back, her chest heaving with rage. "She started it, Rob. She callin' you a deadbeat, sayin' I'm just a side piece."

Rob turned to Latoya, his eyes blazing. "You need to leave, Latoya. Now. This ain't the place for this shit."

Latoya sneered, but she backed down. "This ain't over, Rob. You got responsibilities, and I ain't lettin' you forget that."

As Latoya walked away, Rob turned to Monique, his expression softening. "You a'ight?"

Monique nodded, but the tears spilled over. "No, Rob. I'm not a'ight. I'm tired of this. Tired of fightin', tired of the drama."

Rob pulled her into his arms, holding her tight. "I'm sorry, Monique. I never wanted this for us. I'm gonna fix it, I promise."

The promises were hollow, and Monique knew it. The cracks in their relationship were growing, and she felt like she was losing herself in the chaos.

The following week, Monique sat alone in the apartment, her thoughts a swirling storm of doubt and fear. She heard the door open and close, but she didn't look up. Rob walked over, sitting beside her.

"Monique, we need to talk," he said, his voice serious.

She looked at him, her eyes filled with pain. "What now, Rob?"

"I'm gonna start seein' my kid more. Gonna make sure Latoya can't say nothin' 'bout me bein' a deadbeat," Rob said, his eyes pleading for her understanding.

Monique nodded slowly. "That's good, Rob. But what 'bout us? What 'bout our future?"

Rob took her hand, his grip firm. "We gonna be a'ight. I promise. Just need you to trust me."

Monique wanted to believe him, but the shadows of doubt loomed large. She knew the road ahead would be filled with more drama, more fights, more tears. But she loved Rob, and she wasn't ready to give up on their love.

As the days turned into weeks, Monique tried to find a balance between her love for Rob and the harsh realities of their life. She faced the gossip, the jealousy, the threats, all while trying to hold on to the love that had brought her into this world.

One evening, as Monique sat on the balcony, watching the city lights flicker in the distance, she felt a sense of calm wash over her. She knew their love was tested, but she also knew that love was the only thing keeping them afloat.

Rob joined her, his presence a comforting weight beside her. "You good?" he asked, his voice soft.

Monique nodded, leaning her head on his shoulder. "Yeah. Just thinkin' 'bout us. 'Bout our future."

Rob wrapped his arm around her, pulling her close. "We got this, Monique. We gonna make it through. Together."

As they sat in the fading light, Monique felt a glimmer of hope. Their love was a turbulent storm, but it was also a beacon of light in the darkness. She knew the road ahead would be hard, but she was ready to face it, with Rob by her side.

And as the stars twinkled overhead, Monique couldn't help but believe that, despite the drama, the fights, and the tears, their love would endure. For better or worse, they were in this together, and nothing could tear them apart.

Chapter 8: The Feds Close In

Monique sat on the edge of the bed, her nerves frayed. It had been weeks since she first noticed the black SUV parked down the street, the same one that seemed to follow her every move. She knew what it meant. The feds were closing in, and the walls of their life were starting to crumble.

"Rob, we need to talk," she said, her voice barely above a whisper. Rob was in the kitchen, counting money, his focus on the stacks of cash in front of him.

"What's up, baby?" he replied without looking up.

"That SUV, the one that's always parked outside. I think we're being watched," Monique said, her anxiety clear in her voice.

Rob stopped what he was doing and walked over to her. "You sure 'bout that?"

"Yeah, I'm sure. I've seen it followin' me everywhere. We're under surveillance, Rob. What we gonna do?" Monique's eyes were wide with fear.

Rob sighed, running a hand over his face. "A'ight, I'll handle it. But you gotta stay calm. They lookin' for any reason to bring us down."

Monique nodded, but her paranoia only grew. Everywhere she went, she felt eyes on her. She started to avoid leaving the house, the pressure of constant surveillance wearing on her. She began to question everything, including the man she had married.

One evening, Monique was on the phone with Shanae, her voice hushed. "Girl, I don't know how much more of this I can take. They watchin' us, and Rob actin' like it ain't nothin.'"

"You gotta be careful, Monique. Them feds don't play. They'll find any way to get to Rob, even if it means goin' through you," Shanae warned.

"I know. But I love him. I just... I don't know if I can keep livin' like this," Monique confessed, her voice cracking.

"Just be smart, sis. Watch yo' back," Shanae advised before they hung up.

That night, Monique lay in bed, staring at the ceiling. Rob was beside her, his breathing deep and steady. She wondered how he could be so calm when their world was falling apart. She started to question if she really knew the man she had married, the life she had chosen.

The next day, as Monique was doing laundry, she found a burner phone in Rob's jacket. Her heart raced as she flipped through the messages. They were coded, but she could tell they were about his operations. She felt a surge of anger and fear. Why hadn't he told her about this?

When Rob came home, Monique confronted him. "Why you keepin' secrets from me, Rob? I found the burner phone."

Rob's eyes narrowed. "You goin' through my stuff now? What the hell, Monique?"

"I'm scared, Rob! The feds are watchin' us, and you out here makin' moves without tellin' me. How can I trust you?" Monique's voice shook with emotion.

Rob grabbed her shoulders, his grip firm but not painful. "Listen to me. I'm doin' what I gotta do to keep us safe. You think I want this? I'm tryin' to protect you."

Monique pulled away, tears streaming down her face. "I don't know if I can do this anymore, Rob. This life, it's too much."

Rob's face softened. He cupped her cheek, wiping away a tear. "We gonna get through this, baby. You just gotta trust me."

Monique wanted to believe him, but the doubts gnawed at her. The paranoia, the constant fear, it was all too much. She started to question her choices, the love that had brought her into this dangerous world.

One night, Monique sat on the balcony, the city lights flickering in the distance. Rob joined her, his presence a comforting weight beside her. "You good?" he asked, his voice gentle.

Monique shook her head. "No, Rob. I'm not. I'm scared. I feel like I'm losin' myself."

Rob took her hand, his grip reassuring. "I know it's hard. But we in this together. You and me against the world."

Monique leaned her head on his shoulder, tears spilling over. "I don't know if I'm strong enough for this, Rob. The feds, the danger, it's too much."

Rob wrapped his arm around her, pulling her close. "You stronger than you think, Monique. We gonna make it through. Just gotta stay strong."

As the days passed, the pressure only intensified. Monique felt like she was living in a prison, the walls closing in around her. The feds were relentless, their presence a constant reminder of the danger they were in.

One afternoon, as Monique was walking to the store, she noticed the black SUV again. Her heart pounded in her chest as she quickened her pace. She could feel their eyes on her, the weight of their scrutiny pressing down on her.

When she got home, she found Rob waiting for her, his face grim. "We need to talk," he said, his voice low.

Monique's heart sank. "What's goin' on?"

"The feds, they gettin' closer. I need you to be ready for anything. They might try to use you to get to me," Rob explained, his eyes filled with worry.

Monique felt a surge of fear. "What do you mean, use me?"

"They'll do whatever it takes to bring me down. You need to be careful, Monique. Watch yo' back," Rob warned.

Monique nodded, her mind racing. She knew their time was running out, that the life they had built was hanging by a thread. She started to question everything, including the man she had married.

As the night stretched on, Monique lay in bed, her mind a whirlwind of fear and doubt. She wondered if she had made the right choice, if she was strong enough to survive the storm that was coming.

And as she stared at the ceiling, the weight of their situation pressing down on her, Monique couldn't help but wonder how much longer she could hold on. The feds were closing in, and she felt like she was standing on the edge of a precipice, waiting for the inevitable fall.

The road ahead was uncertain, filled with danger and fear. But Monique knew one thing for sure: she was in too deep to turn back now. She would stand by Rob's side, no matter what, and face whatever came their way.

For better or worse, they were in this together, and nothing could tear them apart.

Chapter 9: The Big Bust

Monique sat at the kitchen table, her mind racing. She knew something was off. Rob had been on edge for days, and now he was gone, handling "business." The paranoia had been eating at her, and she couldn't shake the feeling that everything was about to implode.

The door slammed open, and Rob's right-hand man, Darnell, burst in. "Monique, we gotta move. Now!"

Monique's heart pounded. "What happened?"

"Feds hit one of our spots. They comin' for Rob," Darnell said, urgency dripping from his voice.

Monique's blood ran cold. She grabbed her bag and followed Darnell out to the car. As they sped through the city streets, the sirens wailed in the distance, a grim reminder of the storm that was about to hit.

They arrived at a safe house, a rundown apartment on the outskirts of the city. Monique's phone buzzed incessantly, messages from friends and family, their worry evident in every word. She felt trapped, caught between her love for Rob and the growing realization that their world was crumbling.

Hours later, the news broke. Rob had been arrested in a massive drug bust. The authorities had been watching him for months, building their case. Monique's heart sank as she watched the footage of Rob being led away in handcuffs, his face a mask of defiance.

The door burst open again, this time it was federal agents. "Monique Evans, you're under arrest for conspiracy to distribute narcotics," one of them barked, grabbing her roughly.

Monique's mind went blank. She struggled as they cuffed her, dragging her out of the apartment. The ride to the station was a blur, her thoughts a chaotic whirl of fear and disbelief.

At the station, they threw her into a small, cold room. The walls closed in on her, the gravity of her situation hitting her like a freight train. She was facing serious charges, and the feds weren't playing.

An agent entered, a smug look on his face. "Monique, we know you're not the mastermind here. Help us, and we can help you."

Monique glared at him, her loyalty to Rob burning strong. "I ain't no snitch."

The agent's expression hardened. "You're looking at serious time. Think about your future. Think about what he's dragging you into."

Monique's resolve wavered. She loved Rob, but the thought of spending years behind bars terrified her. She was torn, caught between loyalty and self-preservation.

Days turned into a blur of interrogations and sleepless nights. The feds pressed her, trying to break her down. Monique held on, but the fear gnawed at her, growing stronger with each passing hour.

One night, as she lay in her cell, she thought about her life, the choices she had made, and the love that had brought her to this point. She knew she had to make a decision, and it wasn't going to be easy.

The next morning, they brought her into another interrogation room. The agent sat across from her, his eyes cold and calculating. "So, Monique, what's it gonna be?"

Monique took a deep breath, her heart pounding in her chest. "I need to talk to my lawyer."

The agent smirked, leaning back in his chair. "Smart choice. But remember, time's running out. Make the right decision."

Back in her cell, Monique's thoughts were a turbulent storm. She knew she had to protect herself, but the idea of betraying Rob was a weight on her soul. She had loved him, stood by him through everything, but now she was facing the consequences of that love.

Her lawyer, a sharp-eyed woman named Carla, met with her the next day. "Monique, they've got a strong case. If you cooperate, we might be able to get you a deal."

Monique's heart ached. "I can't turn on Rob. I love him."

Carla sighed, her expression softening. "Love is powerful, but it can't protect you from prison. Think about your future, Monique. Think about your life."

Tears filled Monique's eyes. She was trapped, her world collapsing around her. She had to make a choice, and it was tearing her apart.

That night, as she lay in her cell, Monique made a decision. She would fight for her freedom, but she wouldn't betray Rob. She would find a way to protect herself without turning her back on the man she loved.

The next day, she met with Carla again. "I'll cooperate, but I won't testify against Rob. Find another way," Monique said, her voice steady despite the fear gnawing at her.

Carla nodded, a hint of relief in her eyes. "I'll do my best. But it's going to be a tough fight."

Monique knew the road ahead would be long and hard, filled with challenges and heartbreak. But she was determined to survive, to find a way through the darkness. She had made her choice, and she would stand by it, no matter the cost.

As she lay in her cell that night, the weight of her decision settled on her shoulders. She was in this fight for the long haul, and she wouldn't back down. The feds might have her in their sights, but she was stronger than they knew. And as long as she had hope, she would keep fighting.

The future was uncertain, the path ahead fraught with danger. But Monique was ready to face it, her love for Rob and her determination to survive burning bright in the darkness. She would find a way to navigate the treacherous waters ahead, no matter what it took.

Chapter 10: Prison Blues

Monique sat in the cold, sterile courtroom, her heart sinking as the judge pronounced Rob's sentence. Twenty-five years. The words echoed in her head, a death knell to the life they had built together. She glanced at Rob, his face a mask of stoic resolve. Their eyes met, and in that brief moment, she saw the fear and regret he was trying to hide.

After the sentencing, Monique stood outside the courthouse, feeling the weight of the world pressing down on her shoulders. People stared, whispers and judgmental glances following her like a shadow. She was now marked, forever known as the wife of a drug dealer.

"Girl, you need to stay strong," Shanae said, her voice filled with concern as they walked to the car.

"I know, but it's hard. Everyone lookin' at me like I'm trash," Monique replied, her voice breaking.

"They don't know nothin'. You gotta keep yo' head up, Monique. Rob needs you," Shanae encouraged.

Monique nodded, trying to muster the strength to face the world. She had to keep their life together, for Rob and for herself.

Weeks turned into months, and Monique found herself navigating a maze of legal issues, financial struggles, and the harsh reality of being a drug dealer's wife. She visited Rob as often as she could, their time together limited by prison regulations and the ever-watchful eyes of the guards.

"How you holdin' up, baby?" Rob asked during one of their visits, his eyes filled with worry.

"I'm doin' my best, Rob. But it's hard. People don't let me forget who I'm married to," Monique said, her voice tinged with frustration.

"Don't let 'em get to you. You stronger than that," Rob reassured her, his hand reaching through the bars to touch hers.

"I know. I just miss you so much," Monique whispered, tears welling up in her eyes.

"I miss you too. But we gonna get through this. I promise," Rob said, his voice firm with determination.

Outside the prison walls, Monique faced a different kind of battle. The stigma of being a drug dealer's wife followed her everywhere. At work, she overheard coworkers gossiping about her, their words cutting deep.

"That's her, you know. The one married to that drug dealer," one woman whispered.

"I don't know how she can even show her face around here," another added.

Monique clenched her fists, fighting the urge to lash out. She couldn't afford to lose her job, not with the legal fees and bills piling up. She had to keep her head down and push through the judgment and scorn.

At night, the loneliness was almost unbearable. The bed felt too big without Rob beside her, the silence of the apartment a stark contrast to the life they had shared. She often found herself staring at the ceiling, her mind racing with worries and fears.

One evening, as Monique was walking home from work, she noticed a group of men loitering near her building. She recognized them as members of a rival gang, their eyes narrowing as they saw her approach.

"Yo, look who it is. Rob's girl," one of them sneered, stepping into her path.

Monique's heart pounded in her chest, but she kept her voice steady. "What y'all want?"

"Just lettin' you know we watchin'. Rob might be locked up, but that don't mean you safe," the man threatened, his eyes cold.

Monique swallowed hard, fear gripping her. "I ain't got nothin' to do with his business. Leave me alone."

The men laughed, a harsh, cruel sound. "You part of his life, that makes you part of his problems. Watch yo' back."

They walked away, leaving Monique standing there, her body trembling with fear and anger. She hurried inside, locking the door behind her, her mind racing. She was in constant danger, a target because of her connection to Rob.

As the days passed, Monique struggled to keep her life together. She faced harassment from Rob's enemies, judgment from society, and the ever-present loneliness of his absence. She clung to the hope that they would find a way through this, but the weight of their reality was crushing.

One night, as Monique lay in bed, her phone buzzed with a text from Rob. It was short, but it brought a smile to her face.

Rob: Stay strong, baby. I love you.

Monique replied, her fingers trembling.

Monique: I love you too, Rob. We gonna make it through this.

But as she hit send, a knock on the door shattered the moment. Her heart raced as she got up, peering through the peephole. It was Darnell, his face grim.

"What is it, Darnell?" Monique asked, opening the door.

"Got bad news. Some of Rob's old crew talkin'. They plannin' somethin', and it ain't good," Darnell said, his voice low.

Monique felt a surge of panic. "What you mean?"

"They think you know where Rob stashed some money. They comin' for you, Monique. You need to get outta here," Darnell warned.

Monique's mind raced. She was already on edge, and now this. She had to make a choice, and fast. "Where am I supposed to go?"

"I got a place. It's safe, but we gotta move now," Darnell said, urgency in his voice.

Monique grabbed a bag, stuffing it with essentials. She couldn't believe this was happening. As she followed Darnell out of the apartment, her mind was a whirlwind of fear and determination. She had to stay strong, for herself and for Rob.

As they drove through the city, Monique couldn't shake the feeling that their troubles were far from over. The road ahead was dark and uncertain, but she was ready to face whatever came their way. She had to be. For Rob, for their future, and for her own survival.

Chapter 11: The Rival's Revenge

Monique sat in the dimly lit room, her heart pounding. She had been on the run for days, constantly looking over her shoulder, sleep-deprived and scared out of her mind. She never imagined her life would come to this. But now, a rival gang was convinced she knew where Rob's hidden stash was, and they wouldn't stop until they got it.

Darnell's safe house was small and cramped, the peeling wallpaper and flickering lightbulb adding to the sense of decay. Monique paced back and forth, her mind racing with fear and desperation. She heard footsteps outside and froze, her hand instinctively reaching for the small knife she kept in her pocket.

The door creaked open, and Darnell stepped in, his face grim. "They out there lookin' for you, Monique. We gotta move again."

Monique's heart sank. "Where we supposed to go, Darnell? I can't keep runnin' like this."

"I know, but they serious. If they catch you... it ain't gonna be good," Darnell warned, his eyes filled with concern.

Monique nodded, her body trembling. She grabbed her bag, the few belongings she had left hastily stuffed inside. As they slipped out the back door, she felt the weight of the world pressing down on her. The streets were dark and menacing, the shadows hiding dangers she could barely comprehend.

They moved through the city, sticking to the alleys and backstreets, avoiding the main roads. Every sound, every movement made Monique jump. She felt like a hunted animal, the predators always one step behind her.

As they reached a rundown motel, Darnell checked them in under false names. The room was shabby, the smell of mildew thick in the air. Monique collapsed on the bed, her exhaustion overwhelming her.

"I can't do this, Darnell. I'm losin' my mind," she confessed, tears streaming down her face.

"You gotta stay strong, Monique. Rob needs you to be strong," Darnell said, his voice gentle.

"I don't even know where his stash is! How they expect me to tell 'em somethin' I don't know?" Monique's voice broke with frustration.

"They don't care. They just wanna get to Rob, and they think you the key," Darnell replied, his eyes hardening.

Monique wiped her tears, steeling herself for what was to come. She had to survive, for Rob and for herself. She couldn't let the fear break her.

The next day, as Monique ventured out to get food, she felt eyes on her. She glanced around, her paranoia spiking. A group of men stood at the corner, watching her with predatory gazes. Her heart raced as she ducked into a nearby store, trying to lose them in the aisles.

As she pretended to browse, she heard their voices, low and menacing. "That's her. Rob's girl. She knows where the money is."

Monique's hands shook as she picked up a random item, trying to stay calm. She knew she couldn't stay in the store forever. She had to find a way out, but they were blocking the entrance.

She spotted a side door and made her way towards it, her movements slow and deliberate. Just as she reached the door, one of the men grabbed her arm, his grip like a vice. "Where you think you goin', bitch?"

Monique's fear turned to adrenaline. She lashed out with her free hand, the knife slicing across the man's arm. He yelled in pain, letting go of her. Monique bolted through the door, her heart pounding in her chest.

She ran through the back alleys, her lungs burning, the sound of footsteps behind her. She knew she couldn't outrun them forever. She had to find a place to hide. She ducked into an abandoned building, the darkness swallowing her.

She crouched in a corner, trying to control her breathing, her mind racing with fear and desperation. The men's voices echoed through the building, their footsteps drawing closer. Monique knew she was trapped.

Suddenly, a hand clamped over her mouth, and she was dragged further into the shadows. She struggled, but a familiar voice whispered in her ear. "It's me, Darnell. Stay quiet."

Monique's heart slowed slightly as she recognized him. He led her to a hidden basement, the door blending seamlessly with the wall. They slipped inside, and Darnell bolted the door behind them.

"We safe here, for now," Darnell said, his voice barely above a whisper.

Monique collapsed to the floor, her body shaking with relief and fear. "I can't keep doin' this, Darnell. They gonna kill me."

"I ain't gonna let that happen. We just need to lay low until I can figure somethin' out," Darnell promised, his eyes hard with determination.

Days turned into nights, and Monique's fear and desperation grew. She felt like a prisoner, trapped in a life she couldn't escape. The constant threat of violence, the paranoia, it was all wearing her down.

One night, as they huddled in the basement, Monique broke down. "I can't take it anymore, Darnell. I'm scared all the time. I don't know how to keep goin'."

Darnell sat beside her, his presence a small comfort. "We gonna get through this, Monique. You just gotta hold on a little longer."

Monique nodded, but the weight of their situation was crushing her. She felt like she was losing herself, piece by piece, to the darkness that surrounded them.

As the days dragged on, Monique knew she had to find a way out. She couldn't keep running forever. She needed to take control of her life, to find a way to survive.

One evening, as they were preparing to move to another safe house, Monique made a decision. "Darnell, I need to do somethin'. I can't keep hidin' like this."

"What you talkin' 'bout?" Darnell asked, his brow furrowing.

"I need to confront them. I need to show them I ain't scared," Monique said, her voice steady despite the fear gnawing at her.

Darnell looked at her, his eyes filled with concern. "That's dangerous, Monique. You sure 'bout this?"

Monique nodded, her resolve firm. "I gotta take control of my life. I can't let them keep me in fear."

As they made their way through the dark streets, Monique felt a sense of determination she hadn't felt in a long time. She was ready to face her fears, to confront the danger head-on.

They arrived at a warehouse, the place where the rival gang was known to hang out. Monique's heart pounded, but she kept her head high. She walked in, her eyes scanning the room, her presence commanding attention.

The men turned to look at her, surprise and curiosity in their eyes. The leader, a tall, menacing figure, stepped forward. "What you doin' here, girl?"

Monique met his gaze, her voice steady. "I'm here to tell you I don't know where Rob's stash is. And I ain't gonna let you scare me anymore."

The room fell silent, the tension thick. The leader studied her for a moment, then nodded. "You got guts, I'll give you that. But this ain't over."

Monique held her ground, her fear turning to resolve. "It is for me. I'm done runnin.'"

As she walked out of the warehouse, Darnell by her side, Monique felt a sense of empowerment. She had faced her fears, and she was ready to take control of her life. The road ahead was still dangerous, but she knew she had the strength to survive.

And as the night closed in around them, Monique couldn't help but feel a glimmer of hope. She had taken the first step towards reclaiming her life, and she was ready to face whatever came next. For herself, for Rob, and for the future they had fought so hard to build.

Chapter 12: Betrayal and Deception

Monique sat on the worn-out couch, her mind swirling with doubts and insecurities. The recent threats had left her shaken, but it was the whispers she couldn't ignore. Whispers that Rob, the man she had risked everything for, was cheating on her.

Shanae's words echoed in her mind. "Girl, I heard some shit 'bout Rob. They sayin' he messin' with some other chick."

At first, Monique dismissed it as gossip, the usual drama that came with being married to a man like Rob. But the whispers grew louder, and soon, it wasn't just one name she was hearing. It was multiple. The doubt gnawed at her, consuming her every thought.

She decided to confront Rob during one of their prison visits. She had to know the truth, even if it shattered her heart.

"Rob, we need to talk 'bout somethin' serious," Monique said, her voice trembling.

Rob looked at her, his expression unreadable. "What's on yo' mind, baby?"

"I been hearin' things. People sayin' you been with other women. I need to know the truth," Monique demanded, her eyes burning with anger and hurt.

Rob's face hardened. "Don't listen to that bullshit, Monique. They just tryin' to mess with yo' head."

"Don't play me, Rob. I ain't stupid. I need to know if it's true," Monique insisted, her voice rising.

Rob sighed, running a hand over his face. "I ain't gonna lie to you, Monique. I did some things I'm not proud of. But it don't mean I don't love you."

Monique felt her heart shatter. The man she had stood by, sacrificed for, had betrayed her. "How could you do this to me, Rob? After everything we been through?"

"I made mistakes, Monique. But you gotta understand, this life... it ain't easy. I'm sorry," Rob said, his voice filled with regret.

"Sorry ain't enough, Rob. You broke my heart," Monique whispered, tears streaming down her face.

The visit ended with Monique feeling more lost than ever. She had always known their life was filled with danger and uncertainty, but she never expected to face betrayal from the one person she trusted most.

Back home, Monique couldn't escape the rumors. Women she barely knew would give her pitying looks, some even bold enough to confront her.

"You think you special, Monique? Rob been playin' you. Everybody know it," one woman sneered, her eyes filled with malice.

Monique's fists clenched, her anger boiling over. "Mind yo' damn business. You don't know nothin' 'bout my life."

"Oh, I know enough. You just another one of his playthings," the woman retorted, her words like knives.

Monique stormed away, her heart heavy with pain and anger. She knew she couldn't keep living like this, constantly doubting and second-guessing herself. She had to find a way to deal with the betrayal, to heal from the wounds Rob had inflicted.

One night, as Monique sat alone in their apartment, she heard a knock on the door. She opened it to find Latoya, Rob's ex, standing there with a smug look on her face.

"What you want, Latoya?" Monique asked, her voice laced with annoyance.

"I thought you should know, Rob been messin' with me too. You ain't the only one he playin'," Latoya said, her eyes glinting with satisfaction.

Monique's world tilted. "Why you tellin' me this now?"

"Because you need to see the truth. Rob don't care 'bout nobody but himself," Latoya replied, her voice dripping with contempt.

Monique slammed the door, her mind a whirlwind of emotions. She felt betrayed, used, and utterly broken. The man she had loved, the man she had given up everything for, had been deceiving her all along.

As the days turned into weeks, Monique struggled to find a way to move forward. She felt trapped in a cycle of pain and anger, unable to escape the memories of Rob's betrayal. She withdrew from friends and family, isolating herself in a desperate attempt to heal.

One evening, Monique found herself in front of the mirror, staring at her reflection. She barely recognized the woman looking back at her. The once vibrant, confident Monique was now a shadow of her former self, her spirit crushed by the weight of Rob's deceit.

She knew she couldn't keep living like this. She had to confront Rob one last time, to find closure and reclaim her life.

The next day, Monique visited the prison, her heart pounding with anticipation. She needed answers, and she wasn't leaving until she got them.

"Why, Rob? Why did you do this to me?" Monique asked, her voice trembling with emotion.

Rob looked at her, his eyes filled with regret. "I made mistakes, Monique. I ain't perfect. But I love you. Always have, always will."

"Love ain't supposed to hurt like this, Rob. You broke me," Monique whispered, tears streaming down her face.

"I'm sorry, Monique. I wish I could take it back," Rob said, his voice filled with sorrow.

Monique shook her head, her heart heavy with pain. "I need time, Rob. Time to figure out who I am without you."

As she walked out of the prison, Monique felt a sense of resolve. She was done being a victim, done letting Rob's actions define her. She would find a way to heal, to rebuild her life from the ashes of their broken love.

The road ahead was uncertain, filled with challenges and heartache. But Monique was ready to face it, determined to find herself again. She would no longer be defined by Rob's betrayal. She would rise above it, stronger and more resilient than ever before.

And as she stepped into the sunlight, Monique felt a glimmer of hope. She was ready to take back her life, one step at a time. The journey would be long and hard, but she was prepared to face whatever came her way. For herself, and for the future she deserved.

Chapter 13: The Price of Loyalty

Monique sat in the small, dimly lit interrogation room, her heart pounding in her chest. The walls felt like they were closing in on her, the air thick with tension. She glanced at the door, her mind racing with fear and uncertainty. She had been summoned by the feds, and she knew this was serious.

The door creaked open, and a stern-faced agent walked in, followed by a younger woman with a stack of files. They sat across from Monique, their eyes cold and calculating.

"Monique Evans, you know why you're here," the agent said, his voice low and menacing.

Monique swallowed hard, trying to steady her voice. "Yeah, I know. But I ain't got nothin' to say."

The agent leaned forward, his eyes boring into hers. "You need to understand the gravity of your situation. We're offering you a deal. Testify against Rob, and we'll reduce your charges."

Monique's heart sank. She knew this moment would come, but she wasn't prepared for the weight of it. "I can't do that. I ain't no snitch."

The young woman opened one of the files, sliding a piece of paper across the table. "Look at this, Monique. These are the charges you're facing. Conspiracy to distribute, money laundering, accessory to murder. If you don't cooperate, you're looking at twenty-five years, minimum."

Monique felt her world crumbling around her. The stakes were higher than she had ever imagined. Her loyalty to Rob was being tested in ways she never thought possible. She loved him, but the thought of spending the next twenty-five years in prison was terrifying.

"I love him. I can't betray him like that," Monique whispered, tears welling up in her eyes.

The agent's expression softened slightly, but his voice remained firm. "Think about your future, Monique. Do you really want to throw your life away for him? He's already locked up. He can't protect you anymore."

Monique's mind raced. She knew they were right. Rob couldn't protect her from the consequences of his actions. But the thought of betraying him, of being the reason he spent even more time behind bars, was unbearable.

"I need time to think," Monique said, her voice trembling.

The agent nodded. "You have twenty-four hours. After that, the deal's off the table."

Monique left the interrogation room, her heart heavy with the weight of her decision. She walked through the bustling city streets, her mind a whirlwind of emotions. She had to find a way to navigate this impossible situation, to make a choice that wouldn't destroy her soul.

That night, Monique sat alone in her apartment, staring at the phone. She needed to talk to someone, to get advice, but she didn't know who to trust. She picked up the phone and dialed Shanae's number.

"Hey, girl. What's goin' on?" Shanae answered, her voice filled with concern.

Monique took a deep breath, trying to steady her voice. "Shanae, I need your help. The feds want me to testify against Rob. They say if I don't, I'm lookin' at twenty-five years."

Shanae was silent for a moment, then her voice came through, firm and supportive. "Monique, you gotta do what's best for you. I know you love Rob, but you can't throw your life away for him. He wouldn't want that."

"But if I testify, I'm betraying him. I don't know if I can live with that," Monique said, her voice breaking.

"You gotta think about your future, Monique. You ain't no good to Rob if you locked up too. You gotta find a way to protect yourself," Shanae advised.

Monique knew Shanae was right, but the decision still tore at her heart. She had to find a way to navigate this impossible situation, to protect herself without completely destroying the man she loved.

The next day, Monique returned to the federal building, her heart pounding in her chest. She was led back to the interrogation room, where the agent and the young woman were waiting.

"Have you made a decision?" the agent asked, his eyes focused on her.

Monique took a deep breath, her mind made up. "I'll testify. But I need guarantees. Protection for me and my family. And I ain't gonna lie on the stand. I'll tell the truth, but I won't fabricate no stories."

The agent nodded, a hint of satisfaction in his eyes. "You made the right choice, Monique. We'll make sure you're protected."

As Monique walked out of the federal building, she felt a mixture of relief and guilt. She had made a decision to protect herself, but the cost was high. She knew Rob would never forgive her, and the weight of that betrayal would haunt her for the rest of her life.

The days leading up to the trial were a blur of preparations and anxiety. Monique tried to stay focused, but the emotional toll was heavy. She found herself questioning her choices, wondering if there had been another way.

Finally, the day of the trial arrived. Monique sat in the courtroom, her heart pounding as she took the stand. She glanced at Rob, his eyes filled with a mix of anger and sadness. She took a deep breath and began to speak, her voice steady despite the turmoil inside her.

"I met Rob five years ago. I loved him, and I still do. But I can't lie about what he did. He made choices, and I got caught up in them. I'm sorry, Rob," Monique said, her voice cracking.

As she spoke, she felt a sense of relief and guilt wash over her. She had done what she had to do to protect herself, but the price was high. She knew their love was forever changed, and the weight of that knowledge was heavy on her heart.

When the trial ended, Monique walked out of the courthouse, her mind a whirlwind of emotions. She had made the hardest decision of her life, and now she had to live with the consequences. She knew the road ahead would be difficult, filled with challenges and heartache. But she was ready to face it, determined to rebuild her life and find a way to move forward.

And as she stepped into the sunlight, Monique felt a glimmer of hope. She had survived the storm, and now she was ready to find her own path. The journey would be long and hard, but she was prepared to face whatever came her way. For herself, and for the future she deserved.

Chapter 14: The Snitch

Monique sat in her dimly lit apartment, the weight of her decision pressing down on her. She had agreed to cooperate with the authorities, hoping to secure a better future for herself. The betrayal gnawed at her, but she knew it was the only way to avoid a lengthy prison sentence. The price of loyalty had been too high, and now she had to live with the consequences.

The news spread like wildfire through the streets. Monique was branded a snitch, and the whispers followed her everywhere she went. Her once-familiar neighborhood now felt hostile, the stares and muttered insults a constant reminder of her betrayal.

One evening, as Monique walked to the corner store, she felt eyes on her. A group of men loitered near the entrance, their gazes sharp and unforgiving. She recognized them as Rob's associates, and her heart pounded in her chest.

"Look who it is. The snitch," one of them sneered, stepping into her path.

Monique's throat tightened. "I ain't lookin' for trouble. Just tryna get by."

The man laughed, a cruel sound that sent chills down her spine. "You think you can just walk 'round here like you didn't betray Rob? You got some nerve, girl."

"I did what I had to do," Monique replied, her voice steady despite the fear gnawing at her insides.

Another man stepped forward, his eyes cold and calculating. "People talkin'. You know what happens to snitches 'round here?"

Monique clenched her fists, trying to stay calm. "I ain't got nothin' to say to y'all."

They closed in on her, their presence menacing. Just as she braced herself for the worst, a car screeched to a halt nearby. Darnell jumped out, his face a mask of determination.

"Back off! She's with me," Darnell shouted, his voice cutting through the tension.

The men hesitated, exchanging glances before backing away. "This ain't over," one of them muttered, his eyes filled with hatred.

Darnell grabbed Monique's arm, pulling her towards the car. "You okay?"

Monique nodded, her body shaking. "Thanks, Darnell. I don't know what would've happened if you hadn't shown up."

"We gotta get you outta here. They serious 'bout makin' you pay," Darnell said, his voice tight with worry.

As they drove through the city, Monique's mind raced. She knew she had made enemies, but the reality of the danger she was in hit her like a ton of bricks. She had to find a way to protect herself, to survive in a world that now saw her as a traitor.

Darnell took her to another safe house, a run-down apartment on the outskirts of town. The place was shabby, but it offered a semblance of safety. Monique sank onto the couch, her exhaustion catching up with her.

"Why you doin' this for me, Darnell? You could get in trouble too," Monique asked, her voice barely above a whisper.

"Rob might be pissed, but you still family. I ain't gonna let them hurt you," Darnell replied, his eyes softening.

Monique felt a surge of gratitude, but also a deep sadness. She had lost so much, and the road ahead was uncertain. She knew she couldn't rely on Darnell forever. She had to find a way to protect herself.

Days turned into weeks, and Monique's paranoia grew. Every knock on the door, every shadow in the street, felt like a threat. She stayed inside as much as possible, but the isolation was suffocating. She missed her old life, the sense of community she had once felt.

One night, as Monique lay in bed, she heard a noise outside. Her heart raced as she crept to the window, peering through the curtains. A figure stood in the shadows, watching the building. Monique's blood ran cold. They had found her.

She grabbed her phone and called Darnell, her voice shaking. "Someone's outside. They found me."

"I'm on my way. Stay inside, keep the doors locked," Darnell instructed, his voice urgent.

Monique waited, her mind a whirlwind of fear and desperation. She knew she couldn't keep running forever. She had to confront the danger, to find a way to survive.

When Darnell arrived, they devised a plan. Monique would leave the city, go somewhere they couldn't find her. It was risky, but it was her best chance at a fresh start.

The next morning, Monique packed her belongings, her heart heavy with the weight of her decision. She knew she was leaving everything behind, but it was the only way to stay safe.

As they drove to the bus station, Monique felt a mix of fear and determination. She was stepping into the unknown, but she had no other choice. She had to survive, to find a way to rebuild her life.

At the station, Darnell hugged her tightly. "Stay safe, Monique. I'll keep in touch."

"Thanks, Darnell. For everything," Monique said, her voice thick with emotion.

She boarded the bus, her mind racing with thoughts of the future. The journey ahead was uncertain, filled with challenges and danger. But she was ready to face it, determined to survive.

As the bus pulled away, Monique looked out the window, the city fading into the distance. She felt a pang of sadness, but also a glimmer of hope. She had made her choice, and now she had to live with it.

The road ahead was long and treacherous, but Monique was prepared to face whatever came her way. She would survive, no matter the cost. And as the sun set on the horizon, Monique felt a newfound sense of strength. She was ready to take control of her destiny, to build a future on her own terms.

Chapter 15: A Life in Tatters

Monique sat on the edge of a grimy bed in a run-down motel room, staring at the peeling wallpaper. The room smelled of mildew and stale smoke, a far cry from the life she once knew. Her mind was a chaotic mess of guilt and regret. She had lost everything: her home, her friends, and any sense of security she once had.

A loud knock on the door snapped her out of her thoughts. She tensed, her heart pounding in her chest. "Who is it?" she called out, her voice shaky.

"It's Darnell," came the muffled reply.

Monique let out a sigh of relief and opened the door. Darnell stepped in, his face lined with worry. "You a'ight, Monique?"

Monique shrugged, trying to hold back the tears that threatened to spill. "Just tryna get by, you know?"

Darnell sat down beside her, his eyes scanning the small, dingy room. "You can't keep livin' like this. It ain't safe."

"What choice I got? I got nowhere else to go," Monique replied, her voice cracking.

Darnell sighed, rubbing his temples. "We gotta find a way to get you outta here. This place, these streets... they gonna swallow you whole."

Monique nodded, but the weight of her situation felt crushing. She was trapped in a life she couldn't escape, haunted by the choices she had made. Every night, she lay awake, replaying the past in her mind, the regrets gnawing at her soul.

As the days passed, Monique's situation grew more desperate. She struggled to find work, the stigma of being a snitch following her everywhere. Employers turned her away, their eyes filled with judgment. She was running out of money, and the fear of ending up on the streets loomed over her.

One evening, as she walked through a dark alley, a group of men blocked her path. Their eyes were cold, and their intentions were clear.

"Look who it is. Little Miss Snitch," one of them sneered, stepping closer.

Monique's heart raced. "I ain't lookin' for trouble. Just tryna survive."

"You think you can just walk 'round here after what you did? You a dead woman walkin'," another man spat, his eyes filled with hatred.

Before she could react, they lunged at her, their fists flying. Monique fell to the ground, the pain and fear overwhelming her. She fought back as best she could, but she was outnumbered and overpowered.

As they beat her, she felt a surge of anger and despair. This was her life now, a constant struggle for survival. The streets offered no solace, only pain and violence. Finally, the men left her lying in the dirt, bruised and bleeding.

Monique dragged herself to her feet, her body aching. She stumbled back to the motel, her vision blurry from tears and pain. She collapsed on the bed, sobs wracking her body. She had hit rock bottom, and there was no way out.

The next morning, Darnell found her, his face pale with shock. "What happened to you?"

Monique shook her head, unable to speak. The words caught in her throat, the weight of her despair too much to bear.

Darnell's eyes filled with fury. "We gotta get you outta here, Monique. You can't stay. They gonna kill you."

"But where can I go? I got no one, nowhere," Monique whispered, her voice broken.

"We'll figure it out. But first, we gotta get you patched up," Darnell said, his tone determined.

They moved to another motel, one even more rundown than the last. Monique's wounds were tended to, but the emotional scars ran deeper. She felt like a ghost, drifting through a life that no longer had any meaning.

Every day was a struggle. The guilt and regret haunted her, a constant reminder of the choices she had made. She had betrayed Rob, lost her home, and now she was barely surviving on the streets. She had no one to turn to, no place to call home.

One night, as she sat alone in the motel room, Monique stared at the small, cracked mirror. Her reflection was a stranger, a woman beaten down by life and her own decisions. She felt a surge of anger and determination. She couldn't keep living like this. She had to find a way to take back control of her life.

She reached out to a local shelter, hoping to find some semblance of stability. The people there were kind, but the stigma of her past followed her. She could see it in their eyes, hear it in their whispers.

Still, Monique refused to give up. She started attending support groups, sharing her story with others who had faced similar struggles. Slowly, she began to rebuild her life, piece by piece.

But the streets never let her forget. Every corner, every shadow was a reminder of the danger she was in. Rob's associates still lurked, their threats a constant presence. She knew she had to stay vigilant, to keep moving forward despite the odds.

One evening, as she walked back to the shelter, Monique felt a sense of resolve. She was no longer the woman who had been beaten down by life. She had found a strength within herself, a determination to survive.

But the danger was far from over. She knew the road ahead would be filled with challenges and threats. The streets were unforgiving, and she had to stay one step ahead to survive.

As Monique lay in bed that night, she felt a glimmer of hope. She had been through hell, but she was still standing. The future was uncertain, but she was ready to face it head-on. She would fight for her life, for her survival, no matter what came her way.

And as the night settled around her, Monique knew that she was no longer a victim. She was a survivor, ready to take on whatever the world threw at her. The journey would be long and hard, but she was prepared to face it, one step at a time.

Chapter 16: The Final Confrontation

Monique moved through the dark streets with her head low, every shadow a potential threat. She had been living in fear for too long, the weight of her choices pressing down on her. She had tried to rebuild, but the past never let go, always lurking around the corner, waiting to strike.

She was on her way back to the shelter when she felt it—a cold, sinking feeling in her gut. She quickened her pace, but it was too late. She turned a corner and found herself face-to-face with three of Rob's old associates, their eyes gleaming with malice.

"Well, well, well, look who we got here," one of them sneered, stepping forward. "Little Miss Snitch."

Monique's heart pounded in her chest. "I ain't lookin' for trouble. Just tryna get by."

"Too late for that," another man growled, pulling out a knife. "You think you can just walk away after what you did?"

Monique's mind raced. She glanced around, looking for an escape, but they had her surrounded. "Please, I didn't have no choice. They woulda locked me up forever."

"Choices got consequences, bitch," the first man spat, advancing on her.

Monique backed up until her back hit the brick wall. Fear gripped her, but she knew she had to fight. She couldn't let them end her like this. Not after everything she had survived.

They lunged at her, and Monique ducked, her instincts kicking in. She swung her bag, catching one of them in the face, but the others were on her in an instant. The fight was brutal, their blows landing hard and fast. She struggled, her body screaming in pain, but she refused to give up.

Suddenly, a loud bang echoed through the alley, and the men froze. Darnell appeared, a gun in his hand, his face set in grim determination. "Back off! Now!"

The men hesitated, then backed away, their eyes still filled with hatred. "This ain't over," one of them snarled before they disappeared into the shadows.

Monique collapsed to the ground, her body shaking. Darnell rushed to her side, his eyes filled with worry. "You okay, Monique?"

She nodded, but the tears streamed down her face. "I'm fine... just... tired."

Darnell helped her up, supporting her as they made their way back to the shelter. The reality of her situation hit hard. She had been living in a constant state of fear, always looking over her shoulder, and it had nearly cost her life.

Back at the shelter, Monique sat on her cot, her mind replaying the confrontation. The fear and violence, the look of hatred in their eyes—it was all too much. She felt a deep, aching pain in her chest, a mixture of physical and emotional scars.

"You gotta be more careful, Monique," Darnell said, sitting beside her. "They ain't gonna stop. You gotta lay low for a while."

"I know," she whispered, her voice barely audible. "But I can't keep livin' like this. I gotta find a way to move on."

Darnell nodded, his eyes filled with concern. "I get it. But you need to stay safe. We'll figure somethin' out."

Monique knew he was right, but the weight of her choices felt heavier than ever. She had betrayed Rob, lost everything, and now she was barely surviving. She had to confront her past, to face the decisions that had led her to this point.

That night, as she lay in bed, the memories flooded back. Meeting Rob, falling in love, the dangerous lifestyle, the betrayal, and now the constant fear. She had made choices, and those choices had consequences. She had to find a way to live with them, to move forward despite the pain.

The next day, Monique decided to visit Rob in prison. She needed closure, to confront him and herself. As she sat in the visiting room, waiting for him, her heart pounded with a mixture of fear and resolve.

Rob was led in, his face a mixture of anger and sadness. They sat across from each other, the weight of their shared history hanging in the air.

"Why you here, Monique?" Rob asked, his voice cold.

"I needed to see you. To explain," she replied, her voice trembling.

"Explain what? How you betrayed me? How you ruined our lives?" Rob's eyes burned with anger.

"I didn't have a choice, Rob. They were gonna lock me up forever. I did what I had to do to survive," Monique said, tears streaming down her face.

"Survive? Look at you. You call this survivin'?" Rob spat, his voice filled with bitterness.

Monique nodded, the pain in her chest tightening. "I know I messed up. I know I hurt you. But I can't keep livin' in the past. I gotta find a way to move on."

Rob looked at her, his expression softening for a moment. "I get it, Monique. But you gotta live with what you did. Just like I gotta live with what I did."

Monique nodded, the tears falling freely. "I know. And I'm tryin'. Every day, I'm tryin'."

As their visit ended, Monique felt a sense of closure. She had confronted her past, faced the consequences of her choices. The road ahead was still uncertain, filled with challenges and pain, but she was ready to move forward.

Leaving the prison, Monique felt a newfound sense of resolve. She had been through hell, but she was still standing. She had scars, both physical and emotional, but they were a testament to her strength.

The streets were still dangerous, the threat of Rob's enemies ever-present. But Monique was no longer a victim. She was a survivor, ready to face whatever came her way. She had made her choices, and she would live with them, but she would also find a way to thrive.

As the sun set on the horizon, Monique felt a glimmer of hope. She had faced the final confrontation, and though it had left her scarred and traumatized, it had also made her stronger. She was ready to take on the world, one step at a time. And as she walked into the night, she knew that she was no longer running. She was facing her future head-on, with the strength and determination of a true survivor.

Chapter 17: Picking Up the Pieces

Monique stared at her reflection in the cracked mirror of her small, rundown apartment. She barely recognized herself. The last few years had been a whirlwind of pain, betrayal, and survival. But now, she was determined to rebuild her life from the ashes, even if the road ahead was long and filled with obstacles.

The first step was reconnecting with her estranged family. She knew it wouldn't be easy. They had disapproved of her relationship with Rob from the beginning, and her choices had driven a deep wedge between them. But she had to try. She needed their forgiveness and understanding to move forward.

Monique picked up her phone, her hands trembling. She dialed her mother's number, her heart pounding as it rang.

"Hello?" Denise's voice came through the line, cautious and distant.

"Mama, it's Monique," she said, her voice shaking.

There was a long pause. "Monique. What you want?"

"I need to talk to you. Can we meet? Please?" Monique pleaded, her voice breaking.

Another pause. "A'ight. Come by the house. We need to talk."

Monique hung up, a mix of relief and anxiety washing over her. She got dressed and headed out, her mind racing with thoughts of what she would say. The streets were as unforgiving as ever, the shadows lurking around every corner. But she kept her head high, determined to face whatever came her way.

When she arrived at her parents' house, memories flooded back. The laughter, the warmth, the love she had once known. She took a deep breath and knocked on the door.

Denise opened it, her expression guarded. "Come in."

Monique stepped inside, feeling the weight of her past pressing down on her. Her father, Harold, sat in the living room, his face unreadable.

"Sit down, Monique," he said, his voice stern.

Monique sat, her hands clasped tightly in her lap. "Mama, Daddy, I'm sorry. I know I messed up. I made bad choices, and I hurt y'all. But I'm tryna change. I need your forgiveness."

Denise sighed, her eyes filled with a mix of hurt and love. "We warned you, Monique. We tried to tell you 'bout Rob. But you didn't listen."

"I know. And I regret it every day. But I'm here now, tryna make things right," Monique said, tears streaming down her face.

Harold leaned forward, his eyes intense. "We love you, Monique. Always have. But you gotta show us you mean it. Words ain't enough."

Monique nodded, her heart aching. "I'll do whatever it takes. I just want my family back."

The days turned into weeks as Monique worked to prove herself. She attended counseling, joined support groups, and took on a job at a local diner. It was hard, grueling work, but she found solace in the routine, the small steps toward rebuilding her life.

One evening, after a long shift, Monique sat in the small, cramped apartment she shared with two other women from the shelter. She was exhausted, but the sense of accomplishment was palpable. She had started to piece her life back together, bit by bit.

Her phone buzzed with a message from her mother.

Denise: Proud of you, baby. Keep it up.

Monique smiled, tears welling up in her eyes. She was making progress, earning back the trust and love of her family.

But the streets were still dangerous, and the threat of Rob's enemies loomed large. One night, as Monique walked home from work, she noticed a car following her. Panic set in, but she forced herself to stay calm, quickening her pace.

She ducked into an alley, her heart pounding. The car slowed, and a man stepped out, his face obscured by shadows.

"Monique, you thought you could just walk away?" he hissed, his voice filled with venom.

"I ain't got nothin' to do with Rob no more. Leave me alone," Monique said, her voice steady despite the fear gripping her.

"You think we care 'bout that? You a snitch. Snitches don't get to walk away," he snarled, advancing on her.

Monique's mind raced. She knew she had to fight, to survive. She grabbed a broken bottle from the ground, holding it out in front of her. "Back off!"

The man sneered, but he backed away, his eyes cold. "This ain't over, Monique. You better watch your back."

As he disappeared into the night, Monique's knees buckled, and she sank to the ground, tears streaming down her face. The reality of her situation hit hard. She was constantly looking over her shoulder, always on edge. But she refused to let fear control her life.

She picked herself up and continued home, her resolve stronger than ever. She would not let the past define her. She would keep fighting, keep moving forward.

The next morning, Monique woke up with a renewed sense of purpose. She had faced danger head-on and survived. She was stronger than she ever realized. She spent the day volunteering at the shelter, helping others who were in the same position she had once been. It was cathartic, a way to give back and heal herself in the process.

As the weeks turned into months, Monique's efforts began to pay off. She reconnected with old friends, who were initially wary but eventually welcomed her back. She continued to attend counseling, working through her guilt and regret. Slowly, she started to see a future for herself, one where she wasn't defined by her past mistakes.

One evening, as she sat with her family, sharing a meal and laughter, Monique felt a sense of peace. She had come a long way, but she knew the journey wasn't over. The road to redemption was long and painful, filled with self-reflection and growth. But she was ready for it, ready to keep fighting for her future.

As the sun set on the horizon, Monique felt a glimmer of hope. She had picked up the pieces of her shattered life and was building something new, something stronger. She knew there would be more challenges ahead, but she was no longer afraid. She was ready to face whatever came her way, with her family by her side and a renewed sense of purpose in her heart.

And as she looked around the table, at the faces of those she loved, Monique knew that she was finally on the path to redemption. The future was uncertain, but she was ready to embrace it, one step at a time.

Chapter 18: Til Death Do Us Part

Monique sat in the visitors' waiting area of the prison, her heart heavy with a mix of dread and resolve. This was it, the last time she would see Rob. Their love, once a fiery whirlwind, had become a painful memory, a ghost of what it once was. She knew she had to let go, to finally move on with her life.

A guard called her name, and Monique stood, her legs feeling like lead. She followed him through the cold, sterile corridors until they reached the visiting room. Rob was already there, sitting at a metal table, his face a mask of weariness and regret.

"Monique," he said, his voice carrying the weight of the years they'd spent apart.

"Rob," she replied, forcing a smile that didn't reach her eyes. She sat down, her hands trembling slightly.

There was a heavy silence between them, filled with unspoken words and lingering pain. Monique took a deep breath, trying to steady herself. "I came to say goodbye, Rob. For real this time."

Rob looked at her, his eyes filled with a mix of sorrow and acceptance. "I figured. You look different, Monique. Stronger."

"I had to be," she said softly. "You know I loved you, right? I still do, in a way. But I can't keep holdin' on to the past. It's killin' me."

Rob nodded, his expression grim. "I get it. I did a lot of wrong, hurt you in ways I can't fix. You deserve better."

Monique felt a lump form in her throat. "We both made mistakes, Rob. But I gotta move on, find my own way."

Rob's eyes flickered with something—regret, maybe. "You already started. I can see it in you. You're stronger now, more... whole."

Monique's heart ached. She had dreamed of this moment, but the reality was so much harder. "I'm tryin'. It ain't easy, but I'm gettin' there."

They sat in silence for a moment, the noise of the prison a distant hum. Monique looked at Rob, the man she had once thought she'd spend her life with, and felt a pang of sadness. Their love had been real, but it had also been destructive.

"I want you to know, I forgive you," Monique said, her voice steady. "And I forgive myself too. We both did what we thought we had to do."

Rob nodded, a hint of a smile touching his lips. "Thank you, Monique. That means more than you know."

Tears welled up in Monique's eyes, but she blinked them away. She had cried enough over the years. "Take care of yourself, Rob. I hope you find some peace in here."

"You too, Monique. You got a future ahead of you. Don't let nobody take that from you," Rob replied, his voice filled with earnestness.

Monique stood, feeling a sense of finality wash over her. She had come here to say goodbye, and now it was time to let go. She walked around the table and hugged Rob, a bittersweet embrace that marked the end of an era.

As she pulled away, she looked into his eyes one last time. "Goodbye, Rob."

"Goodbye, Monique. Be safe," Rob said, his voice breaking slightly.

Monique turned and walked out of the visiting room, her heart heavy but her spirit resolute. She had faced her past, confronted her demons, and now she was ready to reclaim her life.

The walk through the prison corridors felt surreal, like a final passage through a dark chapter of her life. She stepped outside, the sunlight hitting her face, a stark contrast to the coldness she felt inside. The world was waiting for her, a world filled with uncertainty but also with possibilities.

Monique took a deep breath, the air feeling fresher, cleaner. She had been through hell, but she had come out stronger on the other side. She knew the road ahead would be challenging, but she was ready to face it head-on.

As she walked to her car, Monique felt a sense of closure. She had said her goodbyes, and now it was time to look forward. The love she had for

Rob would always be a part of her, but it no longer defined her. She was her own person, with her own future to build.

Driving away from the prison, Monique felt a mix of emotions—sadness for what was lost, but also hope for what lay ahead. She had survived the streets, the violence, the betrayals. She had faced her past and found the strength to move on.

Her life was still a work in progress, but she was determined to make it her own. The scars she carried were a testament to her resilience, a reminder of the battles she had fought and won.

As the city skyline came into view, Monique felt a renewed sense of purpose. She was ready to rebuild, to create a life that was hers and hers alone. The journey would be long, filled with ups and downs, but she was ready.

And as the sun set on the horizon, Monique knew that this was just the beginning. She had said goodbye to the past, and now it was time to embrace the future, one step at a time. With each step, she moved closer to the woman she was meant to be, stronger and more determined than ever before.

The end of one chapter marked the beginning of another, and Monique was ready to write her own story, til death do us part.

Don't miss out!

Visit the website below and you can sign up to receive emails whenever Rachael Reed publishes a new book. There's no charge and no obligation.

https://books2read.com/r/B-A-WXARB-OTNUD

BOOKS 2 READ

Connecting independent readers to independent writers.

Did you love *Til Death Do Us Part*? Then you should read *Cartel Bloodline*[1] by Rachael Reed!

Cartel Bloodline: A Tale of Love, Betrayal, and Survival in the Miami Underworld

In the ruthless streets of Miami, where the Cartel controls eighty percent of the cocaine flowing through the port, power is everything, and trust is a luxury no one can afford. When the most feared gangster, Antonio Brown, falls, he leaves behind a legacy that's more explosive than anyone could've imagined. His death unearths a hidden secret—an illegitimate son, Antonio Lewis, who's about to step into a world where loyalty is bought with blood and betrayal lurks around every corner.

Antonio Lewis, raised far from the chaos of Miami's underworld, gets pulled into the Cartel's deadly embrace when he learns of his father's

---

1. https://books2read.com/u/4jpKMk

2. https://books2read.com/u/4jpKMk

empire. Thrown into a cutthroat game where every ally is a potential enemy, Antonio must navigate the treacherous waters of his father's legacy, battling for his place in the empire while uncovering the dark secrets that threaten to consume him.

Lea, a deadly beauty with a heart of steel, leads The Get Money Girls, a crew of contract killers who live by their own rules. When her cousin falls in a botched hit on the Cartel, Lea vows revenge, unaware that her heart would soon become entangled with the enemy. Antonio and Lea's worlds collide in a storm of passion and deceit, their forbidden love a ticking time bomb ready to explode.

As alliances crumble and enemies close in, Antonio and Lea must face the ultimate betrayal from within their ranks. The lines between love and loyalty blur, and survival becomes a deadly game of cat and mouse. The streets of Miami become a battlefield, where every decision could mean life or death, and the only way out is to fight until the last breath.

Will Antonio rise to claim his father's throne, or will the legacy of the Cartel drag him down into the abyss? Can Lea reconcile her thirst for vengeance with the love that binds her to Antonio, or will the secrets they uncover tear them apart forever?

Cartel Bloodline is a gritty, suspense-filled journey through the dark underbelly of Miami, where power is fleeting, love is dangerous, and the ultimate betrayal could come from the person you trust the most. In this world, nothing is as it seems, and the streets never forget.

Also by Rachael Reed

Codefendant
Codefendant
Once a Cheater
Once a Cheater
Passport Bro
What Happens in Prison
Preference
Sprinkle Sprinkle
Championship Bad
Street Exodus
Street Exodus
Street Royalty
Pawns of Power
SIS
Cartel Bloodline
Get Money Girls
Skip the Games
Til Death Do Us Part
Backpage Hustle